PEOPLE AND THE PLANET

Lyn Sirota

Rourke
Educational Media

rourkeeducationalmedia.com

Before Reading:

Building Academic Vocabulary and Background Knowledge

Before reading a book, it is important to tap into what your child or students already know about the topic. This will help them develop their vocabulary, increase their reading comprehension, and make connections across the curriculum.

1. *Look at the cover of the book. What will this book be about?*
2. *What do you already know about the topic?*
3. *Let's study the Table of Contents. What will you learn about in the book's chapters?*
4. *What would you like to learn about this topic? Do you think you might learn about it from this book? Why or why not?*
5. *Use a reading journal to write about your knowledge of this topic. Record what you already know about the topic and what you hope to learn about the topic.*
6. *Read the book.*
7. *In your reading journal, record what you learned about the topic and your response to the book.*
8. *After reading the book complete the activities below.*

Content Area Vocabulary
Read the list. What do these words mean?

carbon monoxide
compounds
gaseous
geothermal energy
global warming
greenhouse gas
hydrocarbons
molecules
particulate
sensing technology
sulfur dioxide
sustainable
thermal
turbines
voltages

After Reading:

Comprehension and Extension Activity

After reading the book, work on the following questions with your child or students in order to check their level of reading comprehension and content mastery.

1. *Why do scientists think Earth's climate is changing? (Summarize)*
2. *What would happen to the planet if pollution was not regulated? (Infer)*
3. *What are "mermaid's tears"? (Asking questions)*
4. *What steps would can you take at home and school to help protect Earth's natural resources? (*Text to self connection)
5. *If all the bees in the world disappeared, how would Earth be affected? (Asking questions)*

Extension Activity

A greater understanding of how human activities affect the planet has led to an increase in "green jobs." Research some existing careers in this category. Then, using what you learned in the book, come up with a few other jobs of the future that could help improve the planet. Be creative—you might just come up with a career you'd like to have someday!

Table of Contents

JUST PEOPLE

The population of the world we live in grows every eight seconds. Earth has more than 7.2 billion people living on it. The United States is the third most populated country in the world behind China and India. Population affects the planet in many ways. Much of the world's air, water, and land are facing a global crisis.

China is the most densely populated country with nearly 1.4 billion people.

China

1 billion +
100 million +
50 million +
25 million +
10 million +
1 million +
< 1 million

The challenge is to create and maintain an effective, **sustainable** way of living that involves preventing **global warming** and climate change; clean air and water; the management of natural and manmade resources to avoid waste; and protecting energy supplies and all living things.

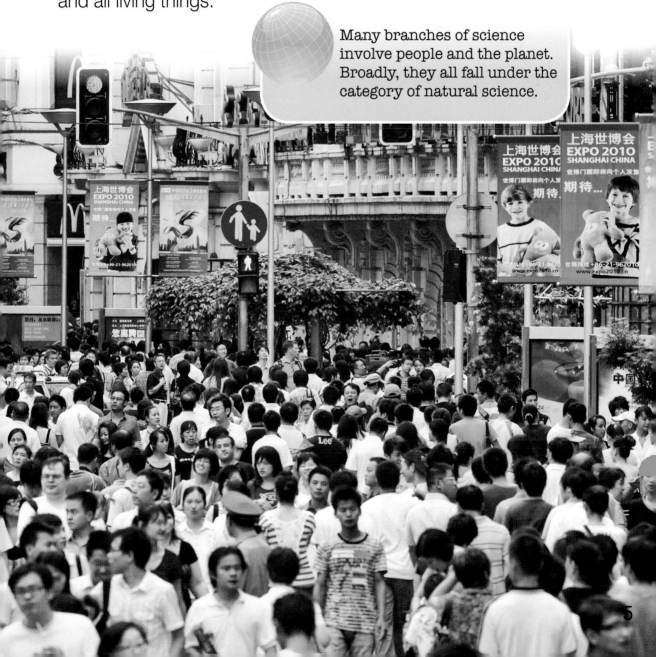

Many branches of science involve people and the planet. Broadly, they all fall under the category of natural science.

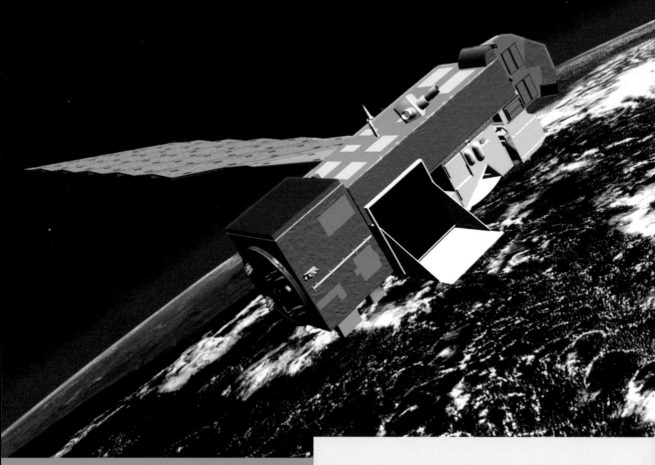

Through remote sensing, Aura spacecraft instruments measure trace gases in the atmosphere. Launched on July 15th, 2004, it studies chemical interactions and climate change in the Earth's atmosphere.

Earth-orbiting satellites and technological advances allow scientists to collect data about Earth and its systems. Much of this data concludes that our planet's climate is changing.

Evidence of Climate Change

- Global sea levels are rising.
- Global temperatures are rising.
- Oceans are warming.
- Ice sheets are thinning and shrinking.
- Glaciers are retreating.
- Precipitation is more intense.
- Ocean water is more acidic.
- Snow in the Northern Hemisphere is melting earlier.

NASA has more than a dozen Earth science spacecraft/instruments in orbit studying all aspects of Earth's systems (oceans, land, atmosphere, biosphere, cryosphere). State of the art research on climate science enables the international scientific community to advance science using space-based observations.

The average temperature in a year is the critical factor for permafrost existence. Permafrost temperatures at 3.3 feet (1 meter) below ground in central Alaska have warmed since the 1960s.

Soil and rock that is frozen all year round is called permafrost. It's found in Alaska, Canada, and other northern countries. While most of the ground is frozen, plants still grow in the soil at the surface.

As temperatures rise, so does the temperature of the ground, which can cause permafrost to thaw or melt. This action affects the land above it. Land may change shape, damaging buildings, roads, and sewer pipes.

Ecosystems are challenged by these changes, too. Thawing permafrost causes changes in lakes and wetlands that provide habitats for birds and water-dwelling animals.

It also changes the supply of wildlife resources for natives who hunt and fish for food. Higher temperatures and less summer moisture increase the risks of drought, wildfire, and insect infestation. Permafrost has carbon trapped inside of it, as well. Thawing causes the release of carbon in the form of a **greenhouse gas** called methane.

Melting sea ice is a bad sign for animals like polar bears that make this their habitat. It also means fewer reflective surfaces in the North to reflect sunlight back into space prompting the planet to absorb more heat.

Weather monitoring instruments aboard special aircraft help us predict hurricanes.

Changing climates also bring about wild weather patterns. Tropical storms and hurricanes get energy from warm ocean water making storms stronger. Hurricanes in the northern part of the Atlantic Ocean have gotten more powerful in the past few decades. The United States has also experienced more intense storms with more rain or snow than in the past.

Though the future is uncertain, change is inevitable. People, government, communities, and companies can use the scientific conclusions to implement changes to provide improvement and better outcomes for an evolving planet.

Fast Fact
Ninety-seven percent of climate scientists agree that Earth's climate-warming trends over the past century are likely due to human activities.

PEOPLE AND THE AIR

People need clean air to breathe in order to survive. The atmosphere is a complex **gaseous** system that supports all life. There are many human activities that pollute the air on the planet. One of the largest sources of air pollution is automobile emissions– something most people use every day!

Pollution from the Internet?!

The world's reliance on the Internet is leading to a rapid increase in greenhouse gas emissions. The energy required to power all the planet's computers, data storage, and communications networks is expected to double by 2020. Growth comes from years of increased energy demands from the world's 30.3 million computer servers and information technology systems.

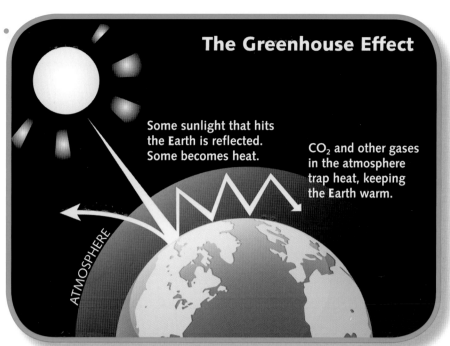

The Greenhouse Effect

Some sunlight that hits the Earth is reflected. Some becomes heat.

CO_2 and other gases in the atmosphere trap heat, keeping the Earth warm.

ATMOSPHERE

Both transportation and factories use fossil fuels such as coal and oil. When these fuels burn, they emit smoke, **sulfur dioxide**, and other **particulate** hazards into the atmosphere. Unburned **hydrocarbons**, **carbon monoxide**, various nitrogen oxides, and ozone are also released. These can react with sunlight to cause smog. Gas emissions such as carbon dioxide trap the sun's energy and heat the Earth, causing a greenhouse effect. This ultimately leads to global warming.

Particulate hazards include soot and ash.

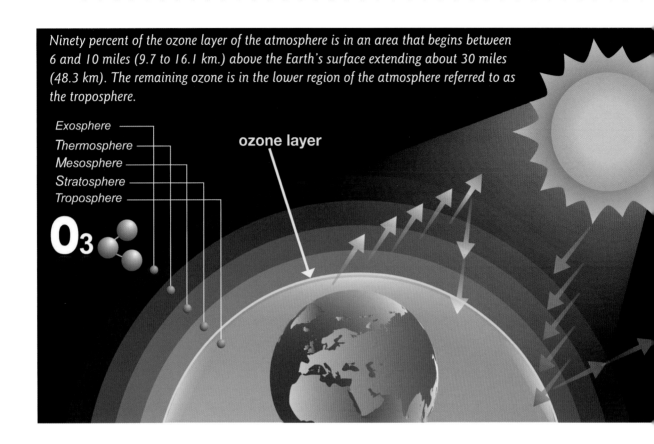

Ninety percent of the ozone layer of the atmosphere is in an area that begins between 6 and 10 miles (9.7 to 16.1 km.) above the Earth's surface extending about 30 miles (48.3 km). The remaining ozone is in the lower region of the atmosphere referred to as the troposphere.

Exosphere
Thermosphere
Mesosphere
Stratosphere
Troposphere

ozone layer

O_3

In the 1970s, government and businesses replaced some products, like aerosol cans, with healthier options.

Chlorofluorocarbons (CFCs) are another form of air pollution. These are chemicals used to clean computer chips. They are also found in cooling devices such as refrigerators and air conditioners. CFCs combine with other **molecules**, attach to ozone, and destroy the protective ozone layer. Ozone acts as a shield from the sun's radiation. It is a form of oxygen that is a pollutant in the lower atmosphere, but beneficial in the upper atmosphere.

Acid rain, a by-product of fossil fuel emissions, is caused by a chemical reaction that begins when **compounds** such as sulfur dioxide and nitrogen oxides are released into the air. These substances rise into the atmosphere where they mix and react with water, oxygen, and other chemicals to form acid rain.

Fast Fact
Acid rain can also be produced from burning coal, volcanic eruptions, and rotting plants.

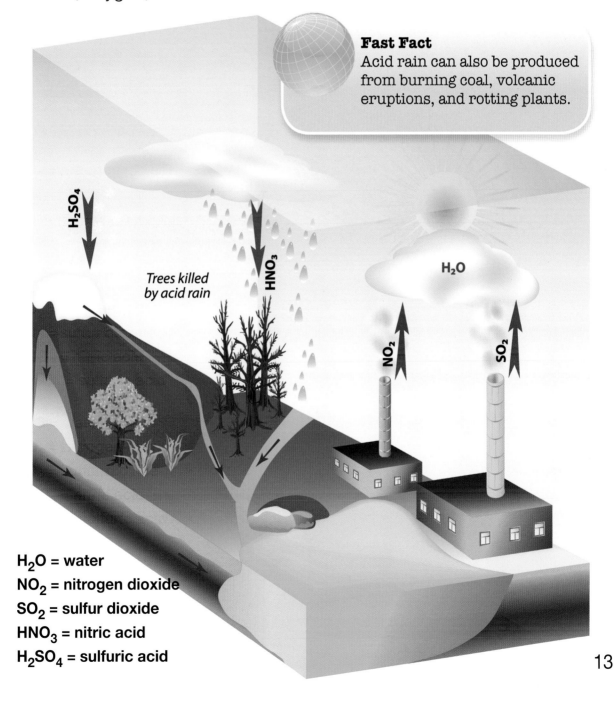

Trees killed by acid rain

H_2SO_4

HNO_3

H_2O

NO_2

SO_2

H_2O = water
NO_2 = nitrogen dioxide
SO_2 = sulfur dioxide
HNO_3 = nitric acid
H_2SO_4 = sulfuric acid

As acid rain flows through soils in a watershed, aluminum is released. This is not only toxic to fish, but causes chronic stress leading to lower body weight and size and making it difficult for fish to compete for food and habitat.

Acid rain is detrimental to all forms of life. In particular, it negatively effects freshwater habitats in lakes, rivers, and streams. Organisms in these habitats cannot survive. Serious effects on human health are also a factor with acid rain. People can inhale particles of sulfur dioxide and nitrogen oxide, which cause respiratory diseases.

Did You Know?

Acid rain is not acidic enough to burn your skin. It generally tastes and smells like normal rain.

Structures made of stone, metal, and cement can be severely damaged by acid rain. Some of the world's greatest landmarks and monuments like the Acropolis in Greece, the U.S. Capitol Building in Washington, D.C., and the Taj Mahal in India have been damaged by acid rain. Steps are being taken to remediate the deterioration and preserve these treasures.

Research has shown that acid rain causes slower growth, injury, or death of forests. It causes changes in buildings and monuments. In exposed areas of buildings and statues, surfaces become rough, material is removed, and carved details become lost.

Clean Power Plan

In 2015, President Obama and EPA Administrator Gina McCarthy released the Clean Power Plan at the White House. It is the most significant climate action ever taken by the U.S. and the first national standards to limit carbon pollution from power plants, which are the largest sources of carbon emissions in the U.S. The Clean Power Plan will reduce carbon dioxide emissions by 32 percent from 2005 levels by 2030.

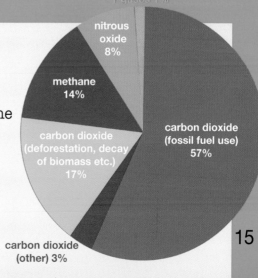

f-gases 1%

nitrous oxide 8%

methane 14%

carbon dioxide (deforestation, decay of biomass etc.) 17%

carbon dioxide (fossil fuel use) 57%

carbon dioxide (other) 3%

Air pollution causes asthma, bronchitis, lung cancer, and other respiratory diseases. The World Health Organization estimates 4.6 million people die each year from causes related to air pollution. Worldwide, this death rate is higher than automobile accidents. Many problems associated with air pollution are directly related to indoor air.

Remove Air Pollutants From Your Home

Using this checklist, scan your home and the products in it. Handle products only to read the labels. Wear plastic or gardening gloves to protect your skin. Always have an adult help you.

1. **Radon** is a radioactive gas that's released when uranium in the soil beneath your home breaks down. Testing kits can be purchased locally.
2. **Carbon Monoxide** is an invisible, odorless gas. Keep furnaces, water heaters and gas ranges in good working order and install a carbon-monoxide detector near bedrooms.
3. **Biotoxins** like molds, bacteria, and dust mites live in your home and can cause allergies, eye irritation, dizziness, and asthma. They thrive in moist areas.
4. **Volatile Organic Compounds (VOCs)** are gases from solids or liquids like fresh paint, lacquer, new carpet, new furniture, wood adhesives, pesticides, and dry-cleaning chemicals.
5. **Pesticides.** Avoid the use of any chemical or synthetic pesticides by selecting disease-resistant plants and washing their leaves. Fertilize them naturally with products derived from animal or plant matter.
6. Household cleaners to avoid:
- **EDTA** and **NTA** (ethylenediaminetetraacetic acid, nitrilotriacetic)
- **Chlorine Bleach.** Also labeled sodium hypochlorite or hypochlorite.
- **Glycol Ethers.** Also labeled ethylene glycol, methoxyethanol, ethoxyethanol, and butoxyethanol.

PEOPLE AND THE WATER AND LAND

About 60 percent of the human body is made of water. Water serves numerous purposes in people, from helping cells, muscles, and skin to hydrating major organs like the heart, lungs, and brain. Fresh water is essential to survival.

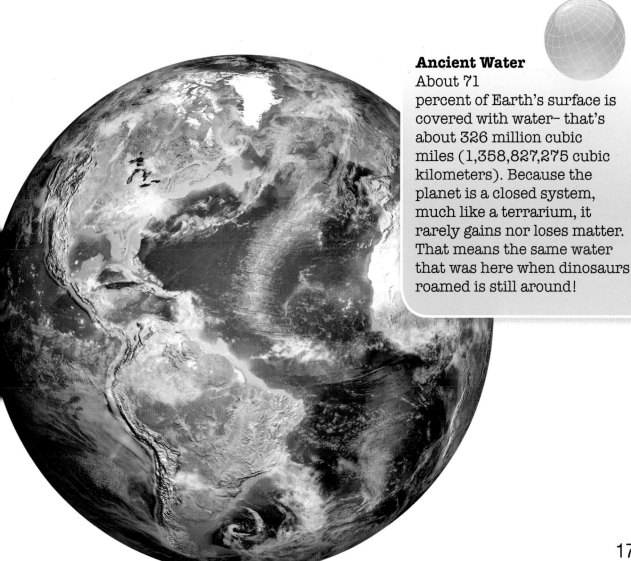

Ancient Water
About 71 percent of Earth's surface is covered with water– that's about 326 million cubic miles (1,358,827,275 cubic kilometers). Because the planet is a closed system, much like a terrarium, it rarely gains nor loses matter. That means the same water that was here when dinosaurs roamed is still around!

Oil from oil spills destroys the insulating ability of furry mammals like sea otters. It changes the water repellency of a bird's feathers and insulation which could cause death from hypothermia.

For many generations, human activities have threatened Earth's water quality. Oceans, rivers, lakes, canals, and streams have been used to carry away waste. Water supplies have been overused. Human activity has also affected other water environments such as groundwater, wetlands, and ice fields. Polluted water cannot be used by people or animals without serious consequences from bacteria and viruses.

Water pollution comes from untreated sewage or human waste. The growing population brings more human waste along with it. In one day, fourteen thousand people die because of contaminated drinking water. Oil and chemical spills wash into waterways and irrigation systems making them unsafe for use. Crop fertilizers and pesticides, radioactive waste, and eroded rock also seep into bodies of water causing contamination and risks for usage.

Depending upon their form and size, plastics can either be ingested, causing internal organ failure, or they can cause a slow strangulation in water dwelling animals. Industry produces an enormous amount of waste, containing toxic chemicals that are dumped into fresh water posing serious problems.

Hydraulic fracturing, known as fracking, is a political and controversial topic that relates to human activity and the planet. Fracking is a process where water, sand, and chemical additives are injected deep into the ground to free up resources such as oil, natural gas, **geothermal energy**, and water trapped in rocks. During this process, natural gas is extracted. There is an environmental advantage of fracking over coal mining, but fracking does, however, add greenhouse gases to the atmosphere.

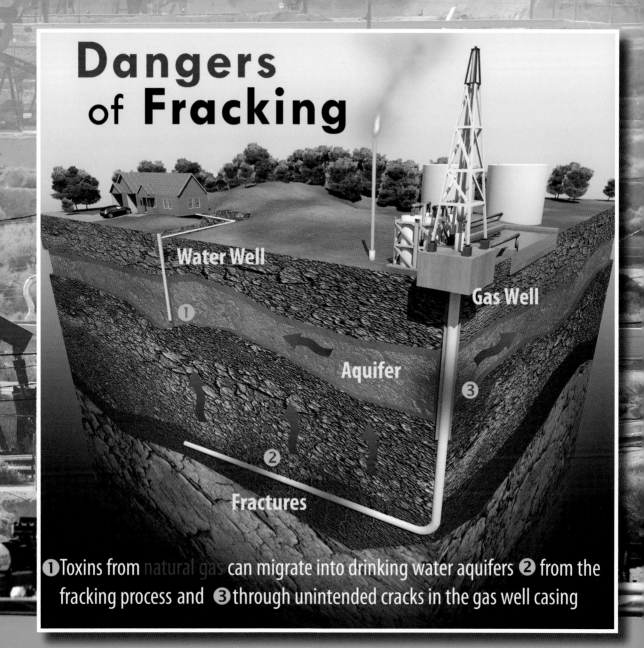

Dangers
of Fracking

Water Well

Gas Well

①

Aquifer

③

②

Fractures

①Toxins from natural gas can migrate into drinking water aquifers **②** from the fracking process and **③**through unintended cracks in the gas well casing

The overuse of land can erode topsoil, which is where plants grow. The soil erosion causes sedimentation of rivers and streams. Particles settle out of water and are carried to other areas of land or water.

Landfills are a source of many chemical substances entering the soil and groundwater environments. Chemicals like lead and other metals leach out of landfill waste.

Backyard burning of garbage creates dioxins, which are highly toxic chlorinated organic chemicals.

21

Chemicals such as farming and agricultural pesticides are a threat to people and the environment. Chlorinated hydrocarbons are an example of a widely used pesticide for mosquitoes that have negative effects on wildlife. Though they have been banned in the U.S., they are still used in other countries and many other pesticides remain in use.

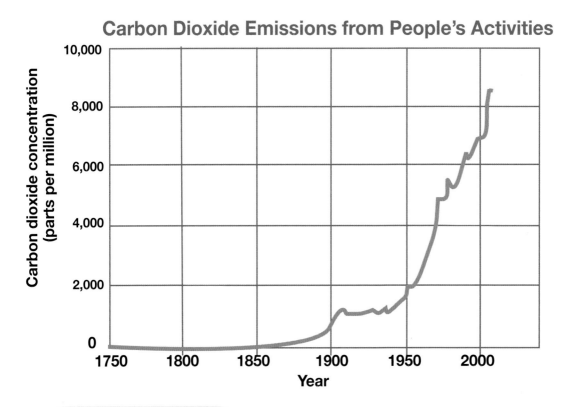

Carbon Dioxide Emissions from People's Activities

SCIENTIST PROFILE

Dr. Dalia B. Kirschbaum, Water-Cycle Scientist at NASA Goddard Space Flight Center, is a research physical scientist in the Hydrological Sciences Lab at NASA Goddard Space Flight Center in Maryland. Her current research is focused on landslide hazards and forecasting. She is also developing remote **sensing technology** in the awareness of landslide hazards. Dr. Kirschbaum received her M.S. and Ph.D. in Earth and Environmental Sciences from Columbia University with a focus in Natural Hazards and Remote Sensing. She received her A.B. in Geosciences from Princeton.

Make Your Own Organic Garden

What You'll Need

- wooden box, 1.5 to 2 feet (.5 to .61 meters) deep; 3 to 4 feet (.9 to 1.2 meters) wide
- fresh garden soil (chemical free)
- small pebbles
- drill (to be used with an adult)
- fruit or vegetable seeds, or plants

What You'll Do

1. Clean the wooden box and make 5 or 6 small holes at the bottom for the water to drain out.
2. Cover the holes in the box by using small pebbles, but be careful not to block the drainage holes.
3. Put soil in box.
4. Plant the fruit or vegetable seeds or plants in the soil. Keep some distance between plantings to allow space to grow.
5. Water your seeds or plants regularly and make sure they are not getting too much sun or rain.
6. Check the drainage regularly to make sure it doesn't get blocked. Enjoy the fruits or vegetables of your labor!

PEOPLE AND RENEWABLE ENERGY

Nonrenewable energy comes from sources that will run out or will not be replenished in our lifetime or in many lifetimes. Most nonrenewable energy sources are fossil fuels like coal, petroleum, and natural gas. Carbon is the main element in fossil fuels.

With the many changes in the world since the Industrial Revolution, renewable energy has become the norm rather than a trend. Investments in new technologies have expanded significantly. Between 2013 and 2015, the U.S. and Europe have added more power from renewable energy than from coal, gas, and nuclear combined.

Biomass, solar, and wind technologies have had significant growth. Biomass ferments or burns plant material to generate electricity. Solar utilizes **thermal** panels to convert the sun's radiation into heat. Wind **turbines** that vary in size generate electricity. Other sources that generate electricity are geothermal, hydro, tide, wave, and ocean energy.

Examples of nonrenewable energy

coal

oil
petroleum

natural gas

Examples of renewable energy

biomass

solar

wind

Scientists have recently reported on new devices that generate power from other forces in nature. Evaporation is a powerful force that pulls water from the Earth. It was discovered that evaporation can power both a floating engine and an engine that drives a small car.

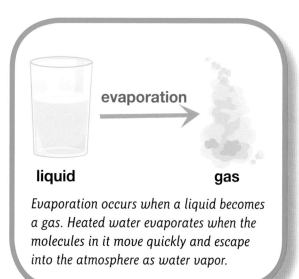

evaporation

liquid   gas

Evaporation occurs when a liquid becomes a gas. Heated water evaporates when the molecules in it move quickly and escape into the atmosphere as water vapor.

Photovoltaics are solar cells flexible enough to provide electricity for communities. Solar cells are connected to each other and mounted in a frame called a module. Modules can supply electricity at specific **voltages**.

The Freiburg Solar Settlement is Europe's most modern residential and commercial development project. It is an energy sustainable dwelling designed to reduce consumption to a minimum.

Biodiesel is a renewable, biodegradable fuel that can be manufactured from vegetable oils, animal fats, or recycled restaurant grease. It is a cleaner-burning replacement for petroleum diesel fuel.

Biodiesel fuels are also a growing alternative in reducing emissions. Biodiesel fuels are clean burning replacements to diesel made from agricultural oils, recycled cooking oil, and animal fats. These fuels are produced in nearly every state of the country.

Cows expelling methane gas is no laughing matter! Studies estimate that converting cow manure from the 95 million animal units in the United States will produce renewable energy equal to 8 billion gallons (30,283,294,272 liters) of gasoline. This adds up to one percent of the total energy consumption in the nation and makes a good dent in pushing aside fossil fuels.

Much of the success of this source is reliant on electricity prices and what is paid for converted energy. In addition, financial support from the government and other sources is necessary to fund this.

Burps vs Farts

The second most common greenhouse gas emission is methane. Cows produce more than milk; they also produce methane. Which do you think is a bigger methane source: cow

Make Solar S'mores

What You'll Need
- cardboard box, at least three inches (7.6 centimeters) deep with attached lid; the lid should have flaps so that the box can be closed tightly.
- aluminum foil
- clear plastic wrap
- glue stick
- tape (any type)
- stick to prop open reflector flap
- ruler
- box cutter or X-acto knife (USE ONLY WITH ADULT)

What You'll Do
1. Using the ruler, cut a three-sided flap out of the top of the box. Leave at least a 1-inch (2.54 centimeter) border around the three sides.
2. Cover the bottom (inside) of the flap with aluminum foil. Spread a coat of glue from the glue stick onto the cardboard first and smooth out the foil.
3. Line the inside of the box with aluminum foil.
4. Tape two layers of plastic wrap across the opening you cut in the lid—one layer on the top, one layer on the bottom side of the lid.

burps or cow farts? Burps it is! This is because more methane is produced during the digestive process, where sugar is converted into simple molecules for absorption into the bloodstream.

Renewable energy is producing positive change and growth in stabilizing emissions of carbon dioxide and other greenhouse gases. Every change is a positive step toward cleaning up the planet.

5. Prop the lid up with the stick. You may have to use tape.
6. Put the oven in direct sun, with the flap propped to reflect the light into the box. Tape the prop in place if necessary. Preheat oven for 30 minutes.

For Solar S'mores, You'll Need
- graham crackers
- large marshmallows
- plain, thin chocolate bars
- aluminum pie pan
- napkins

With the help of an adult

1. Break graham crackers to make squares. Put four squares in the pie pan. Put a marshmallow on each.
2. Place the pan in the preheated oven.
3. Close the oven lid (the part with the plastic wrap) and prop up the flap to reflect the sunlight into the box.
4. The marshmallows should get mushy in 30 to 60 minutes.
5. Open the oven lid. Put a piece of chocolate on top of each marshmallow. Put another graham cracker square on top of the chocolate. Press down.
6. Close the oven lid. Let the sun heat it for a few more minutes and, presto! Your s'mores are ready.

PEOPLE, POLLUTION, AND THE PLANET

The commitment to improving the planet's condition is an international effort. Most nations have signed international agreements that involve local government, small businesses, corporations, civil and religious organizations, and even municipalities. Many countries have signed the United Nations (UN) Framework Convention on Climate Change (UNFCCC), which requires nations to reduce their own emissions. They are also asked to finance other countries' research to implement change. The goal is to stabilize greenhouse gas concentrations within a set timeframe.

Human advances in technology have brought the world faster computers and cell phones. However, that comes along with hazardous e-waste of toxic materials. Though some of it can be recycled, it also ends up in landfills.

The Environmental Protection Agency reported in 2013, the average American household uses about 28 electronic products. With this increased supply of new gadgets, Americans generated 3.14 million tons of electronic garbage.

Scientists are concerned that humans have added radiation to the environment. Testing nuclear weapons and disposing nuclear waste safely is dangerous and expensive.

Some forms of radiation are found in the natural environment and others are due to modern technology. Exposure to radiation is measured by Geiger counters and similar devices. A Geiger counter converts scientific information into an electronic signal.

Thermal imaging cameras translate thermal energy (heat) into visible light to analyze an object or scene.

Heat or thermal pollution is a result of the increased energy needs of people. When heat is added to bodies of water, temperatures rise and animals' environments change drastically.

Noise and light pollution have an impact on the planet, as well. Research links noise pollution with stress-related illnesses, sleep disturbances, high blood pressure, speech interference, and hearing loss.

Light pollution not only affects animals and their migration patterns, but over-illumination wastes about two million barrels of oil per day.

The decisions people make about how and where communities are built have significant effects on the natural environment and on human health. Construction sites create waste and contribute to noise pollution. Building and transportation decisions need to be made with consideration of the environment.

Light pollution is a by-product of humans lighting objects or areas at night with misdirected or shielded sources. Light is pointed up to the sky rather than down to the earth.

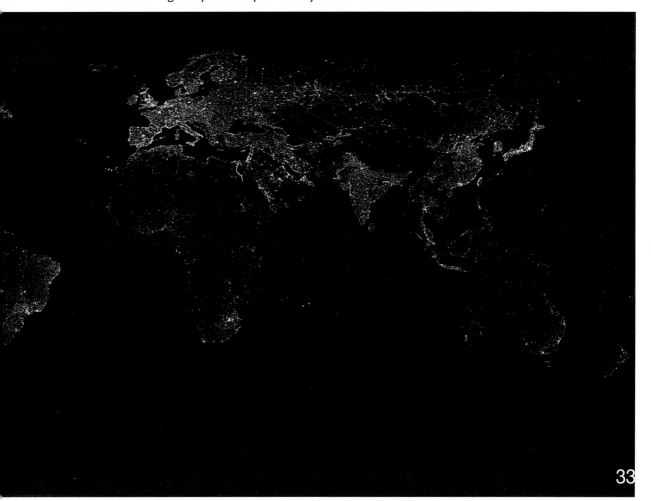

Natural disasters have profound effects on the planet. Hurricanes contaminate water from sewage. Earthquakes affect agricultural production and irrigation systems. Tornadoes destroy crops and farms. Tsunamis cause flooding and fires from gas lines and damaged tanks. All events in nature are a cycle. They change the environment and come back to change the lives of people.

Fukushima Nuclear Accident

In March of 2011, an earthquake and several tsunami waves hit the east coast of Japan causing immense damage. At the Fukushima nuclear power plant, the power supply cooling system were impacted. Reactors melted down and hydrogen gas exploded. People had to be evacuated and relocated. An unpredictable disaster led to a predictable disaster.

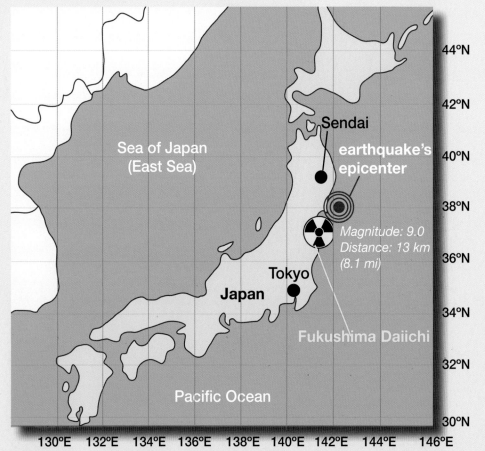

A seismograph provides us details about an earthquakes location and depth.

Earthquake damage from Japan, 2011.

Humans have become efficient at using technology to predict natural disasters on Earth. However, not all catastrophic events can be predicted.

Earthquakes can strike at any moment wreaking havoc on the environment. They destroy homes and businesses and can kill people by the thousands. They can also trigger additional disastrous events like tsunamis and fires.

Tsunami Warning Centers provide early detection and warnings for potentially dangerous tsunamis.

As technology advances, we may someday be able to determine, when and where man-made or natural disasters will occur.

ANIMAL HABITATS AND THE PLANET

From ponds to oceans and bushes to forests, Earth is home to at least 13 billion animal and plant species. Wildlife is profoundly altered by sudden changes caused by human activity. Clearing land to build roads and to grow crops, pollution from industry, and farming threaten the survival of plants and animals. With the world's population on the rise, farming and food production will need to meet these changing demands.

Fast Fact
Earth's population is projected to reach three billion by 2040.

Fossil fuels release massive amounts of carbon dioxide into Earth's atmosphere, warming up ecosystems and threatening the natural environment. Buildings benefits humans, but changes life for animals. Construction can cause animals to change their movement patterns and can prompt them to move into areas where people are living.

Construction disrupts and forces animals out of their natural habitats. Loss of habitat is the primary threat to the survival of wildlife in the United States.

Rainforests are one of Earth's richest and most diverse sources of plant and animal species. Forests play a role in the natural process of storing carbon while providing habitats for many species. People are burning and clearing forests for their trees and to grow crops, which causes deforestation. When the trees are taken down, it causes an "edge effect."

Fast Fact
The edge effect is the end result of deforestation. Protection from the elements like heat and wind are lost, creating exposure and vulnerability to drought and fires.

The forest is harshly exposed to wind, light, and drier air. Drier air causes forest fires. The climate changes for animal species in and around the forest. In some cases it brings in invasive species. Invasive species are not native to the ecosystem and can cause harm. They can be plants, animals, or other organisms.

Perhaps one of the greatest environmental challenges brought on by human activity is desertification. Desertification happens when plants or trees that bind soil are removed, erode, or are farmed. This removes the nutrients in the soil. Wind and water erosion make it worse, moving topsoil and leaving behind a mix of dust and sand that isn't fertile for growing.

Human exploitation of land leads to desertification. This causes soil to erode and change and fragile ecosystems suffer as an end result.

Desertification begins in areas that are dry or suffer from drought and can spread into other areas. It is devastating to vegetation and animals causing irreversible changes to ecosystems. Many animal species must migrate to other areas to find food, water, and shelter or risk endangerment.

Areas of the world that are rich with animal and plant life are having to manage human activity while balancing events like wildfires and droughts. Rising sea levels are destroying low-lying habitats. Whether they are land or water, ecosystems rely on the relationships between species and the environment, so even small changes will have large consequences.

The Buzz on Bees

Global warming is causing a decline in the bumblebee species and their habitats. Researchers examined more than 420,000 historical and current records of many species of bumblebees and confirm their decline due to climate change. Bumblebees pollinate plants that provide food for humans and other animals so this is a concern. Research found that the bees are moving to habitats at higher elevations due to climate change. Because of this, researchers are considering "assisted migration" of the bees to new areas where they can thrive.

Bees pollinate about 70 of our 100 major crops, including broccoli. However, these critical pollinators are dying - 42% of U.S. bee colonies collapsed in 2015.

BALANCING THE PLANET

Keeping the planet in balance requires many things. Some key solutions involve advanced technology to reduce greenhouse gas emissions, reducing and minimizing climate change, reducing risks, managing resources and world strategy/action. All of this needs to take place within a timeframe that will allow ecosystems to naturally adapt to change. Food production also needs to be managed so it isn't affecting the economy.

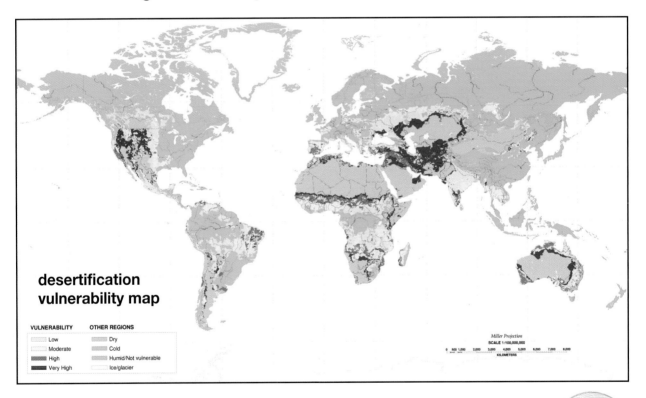

desertification vulnerability map

VULNERABILITY	OTHER REGIONS
Low	Dry
Moderate	Cold
High	Humid/Not vulnerable
Very High	Ice/glacier

Miller Projection
SCALE 1:100,000,000

0 500 1,000 2,000 3,000 4,000 5,000 6,000 7,000 8,000
KILOMETERS

World Desertification

According to the United Nations, 52 percent of land used for agriculture is affected by desertification. This affects 1.5 billion people around the world. Loss of land is currently happening at 30 to 35 times the historical rate. Worldwide desertification impacts biodiversity, the economy, and sustainability.

People need to make changes for sustainability. From the way homes are run to recycling, conservation, and car usage, all lifestyle changes can benefit the planet. Even turning the heat down and the air conditioning up can have positive effects. Reusing things, taking shorter showers, and getting creative around the house can add many benefits. Being carbon conscious involves making decisions every day.

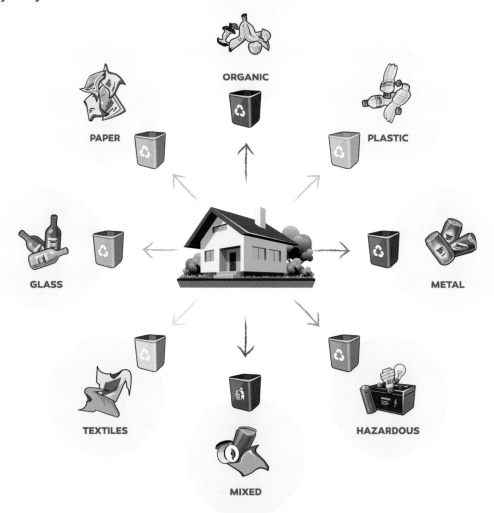

According to the EPA, the national recycling rate is at 30%. Increasing this to 60% through education and communication could save the equivalent of 315 million barrels of oil per year.

Adapting to life in a changing climate requires flexibility. For example, farmers must adapt to extended growing seasons made possible by warmer climates. Communities need to work together to plan for extremes, protect energy, build flood prevention systems, plan for heat waves and high temperatures, and improve water storage and use.

The overall effects of not taking action or taking action too slowly will come back to affect people. Americans are exposed to unhealthy levels of ozone and particle pollution. Approximately 3.9 million children and over 10.7 million adults live in the United States with high ozone levels. Over 5.4 million people have chronic bronchitis and emphysema.

Make a Better Footprint

With an adult's help, calculate your carbon footprint on the Environmental Protection Agency (EPA) website:

www3.epa.gov/carbon-footprint-calculator/

The calculator will estimate your footprint based upon your home energy, transportation, and waste. Like fingerprints, footprints vary depending upon location, habits, and personal choices. To pinpoint an even closer estimate, gather data from your utility bills.

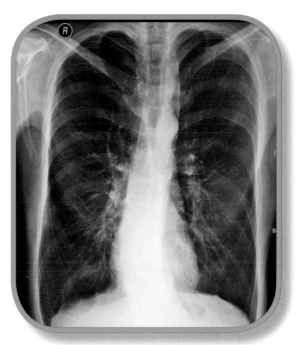

Ozone is a powerful oxidant that can irritate airways and aggravate lung issues such as bronchitis and emphysema.

With permission, take action right now! Track your school's climate impact by making a list of the school's greenhouse gas emissions. Figure out productive ways to make changes and create an action plan that can be presented to your teacher, principal, or other administrative employees. The same thing can be done in your own house. Positive changes and action steps can be presented to parents and families can make changes together.

Philadelphia's Magic Gardens.
All art by Isaiah Zagar. Photography by Emily Smith

Taking action can be signing a beneficial petition, or many petitions, that protect the world's natural resources. There are so many ways to get to green! Any positive action toward a better planet is more than no action.

"Don't judge each day by the harvest you reap, but by the seeds you plant."

-Robert Louis Stevenson

Getting Creative

Using garbage to make art is one of many examples of how people can get creative when it comes to recycling and conservation. Philadelphia's Magic Gardens (PMG), in Philadelphia, Pennsylvania, is a great example of putting this idea into action. The artist behind PMG, Isaiah Zagar, aims to inspire creativity and educate the public about folk, mosaic, and visionary art. PMG exhibits a mosaic art environment and public murals.

GLOSSARY

carbon monoxide (kar-buhn muh-NOK-side): a poisonous gas produced by the engines of vehicles

compounds (kom-poundz): things formed by combining two or more parts

gaseous (gash-uhss): a substance such as air that will spread to fill any space that contains it

geothermal energy (jee-oh-thur-muhl en-ur-jee): power from the intense heat of the Earth to make machines work and produce heat

global warming (glohb-uhl wor-uhm-ing): an apparent gradual rise in the Earth's atmosphere caused by the greenhouse effect

greenhouse gas (green-houss gass): gases such as carbon dioxide and methane that are found in the Earth's atmosphere and help hold heat in

hydrocarbons (hye-droh-kar-buhnz): a substance that contains only carbon and hydrogen

molecules (mol-uh-kyoolz): the smallest part of a substance that contains all the chemical properties of the substance

particulate (par-ti-KUHL-ate): matter in particle form

sensing technology (senss-ing tek-nol-uh-jee): the use of instruments to gather data which, at times, may be gathered from a distance

sulfur dioxide (suhl-fur dye-ok-side): a poisonous gas found in some industrial waste which causes air pollution

sustainable (suh-stayn-uh-buhl): to keep something going

thermal (thur-muhl): holding in heat

turbines (tur-binez): an engine driven by water, steam, or gas passing through the blades of a wheel and making it revolve

voltages (vohl-tij-uhz): forces of electrical currents expressed in volts

INDEX

SHOW WHAT YOU KNOW

1. Provide evidence of climate change. List at least three ways the climate is changing.
2. What suggestions do you have to help areas that are affected by desertification?
3. What's an example of a chemical that negatively affects the environment? Explain its effect.
4. What is the difference between renewable and nonrenewable energy sources?
5. Describe some ways human activities are affecting animals and their ecosystems.

WEBSITES TO VISIT

www.worldwildlife.org/species

www.climatekids.nasa.gov

www.epa.gov/climatestudents

ABOUT THE AUTHOR

Lyn Sirota has written many science and nature books, articles and poems for children. She spends her days writing, teaching and practicing yoga, and volunteering in local schools and animal shelters. Lyn lives in central New Jersey with her husband, children and three furry rescues. For more information about her, visit her website: www.lynsirota.com and blog: http://blog.lynsirota.com.

Meet The Author!
www.meetREMauthors.com

© 2016 Rourke Educational Media

www.rourkeeducationalmedia.com

PHOTO CREDITS: Cover and title page: cityscape © kwest, smoke stacks © Olegusk, crowd © blvdone, windmill © stocknadia; page 4 map © Hadrianoliver~enwiki, photo page 4-5 © TonyV3112; page 6-7 courtesy of NASA, page 7 top NASA/JPL-Caltech, bottom left © Adwo, bottom right © R. Vickers; page 8 © Dimos, page 9 © MISHELLA; page 10 © Hung Chung Chih, page 11 bottom photo © Dennis Albert Richardson; page 12 © Crystal-K, page 12 spray can © Kar, page 13 © Designua; page 14-15 river © Jose Arcos Aguilar, bottom left © Mary Terriberry, bottom right © Laurence Gough; page 15 pie chart source: EPA; page 17 © NPeter; page 18-19 oil spill © jukurae / Shutterstock.com, page 19 bottom left © overdrew; page 20-21 © Christopher Halloran / Shutterstock.com, page 21 diagram © AuntSpray, page 25 top left © BarryTuck, middle © huyangshu, top right © Chepko Danil Vitalevich, bottom left © stocksolutions, middle © Vaclav Volrab, bottom right © WDG Photo; page 26 top © snapgalleria, bottom © Andrewglaser; page 27 © ThamKC; page 30-31 © Huguette Roe, page 31 top left © overdrew, top right © wellphoto; page 32 © Ivan Smuk, page 33 earth light image Data courtesy Marc Imhoff of NASA GSFC and Christopher Elvidge of NOAA NGDC. Image by Craig Mayhew and Robert Simmon, NASA GSFC; page 34 © Roulex_45, page 35 top courtesy of NOAA, bottom © gentlemanrook; page 36-37 © page 37 fox photo © Jamie Hall; page 38-39 © sittitap, page 39 inset photo © Dirk Ercken; page 40 © bourbon, page 41 map USDA; page 42 © petovarga; page 43 © Hong xia

Edited by: Keli Sipperley

Cover and Interior design by: Nicola Stratford   www.nicolastratford.com

Library of Congress PCN Data

People and the Planet / Lyn Sirota
(Let's Explore Science)
 ISBN 978-1-68191-396-4 (hard cover)
 ISBN 978-1-68191-438-1 (soft cover)
 ISBN 978-1-68191-477-0 (e-Book)
Library of Congress Control Number: 2015951563

Also Available as:

Printed in the United States of America, North Mankato, Minnesota